This book belongs to:

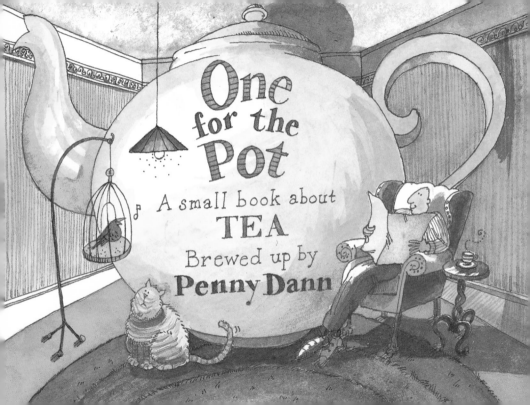

One for the Pot

A small book about
TEA

Brewed up by

Penny Dann

First published in Great Britain 1985
by Elm Tree Books/Hamish Hamilton Ltd
Garden House 57-59 Long Acre London WC2E 9JZ

British Library Cataloguing in Publication Data

Dann, Penny
    One for the pot.
    1.Tea — Social aspects — Great Britain
    I. Title
    394.1'2   GT2907.G7

    ISBN 0-241-11691-0

Printed in Great Britain by
Cambus Litho Ltd, East Kilbride.

For
J.D.
With
love

TWININGS

EST. 1706

TEAMEN TO CONNOISSEURS
FOR OVER 275 YEARS

Major Robert Bruce discovered Camellia Sinensis growing wild in India in 1823. The tea-bush was very soon under intense cultivation. Estates were established in 3 main areas.

These are:

Nilgiri - This tea is grown in a very beautiful mountainous region of South India. It is a mild flavoursome tea, that is harvested all year round.

Assam - This, the largest and most productive growing area in the World is situated in the North East of India in the Valley of the Brahmaptura River. Millions of kilos of tea are grown here each year. Assam tea produces a strong and pungent liquor.

Darjeeling - This tea area is also in the North East, amongst the foothills of the Himalayas. It has earned the name 'Champagne of Teas'

The combination of elevation, bush, soil and relative scarcity make it the most highly prized of all Indian teas.

The first Indian tea was sold in Britain in 1839. The strong links that Britain held with India helped to quench the tea-thirst of the British population, and make tea-drinking a national institution.

The technique of plucking is to nip the top two leaves and the bud from each stem. An expert tea-plucker can gather 150lb in a single day! enough to make 37lb of black tea.

zzzzzzz

During the 17th Century tea was rare and expensive. The small amounts of tea that reached Britain through the East India Company were subject to heavy taxes. Smugglers seized the opportunity to supply a growing demand.

Tea-smuggling did indeed become a big business, but one had to be wary of the odd rogue, who would try to pass off used tea that had been treated and dried, or mixed with 'fillers' such as dried liquorice leaves. Even animal dung was used!

There were over 2,000 Coffee-houses in London by 1700. Thomas Twining took over "Tom's Coffee House" in the Strand in 1706. In a bid to gain more business he began to sell dry tea. It proved to be a very successful venture, and Twining's Company began to supply other retail outlets, and abroad.

One of Thomas Twining's successors, Richard (1749 – 1824), campaigned against the bad system of tea importation, the smuggling and the taxes. He succeeded and in 1784 the price of tea was halved.

Tea went on to overtake coffee in popularity amongst both the rich and the poor.

In the home, tea was stored in secure containers to keep out the servants! The key was guarded by the lady of the house. Tea caddies were made from precious woods and metals. Some contained several sections, to hold different teas, a caddy-spoon, and a small bowl in which to blend the teas to suit.

Several stories are told of the discovery of tea. Probably the earliest claim was made by the Emperor Shen-Nung of China, 5,000 years ago!

The event was a happy accident, a few leaves from a common shrub, camellia sinensis, fell into the pot of water he was boiling. He found the resulting infusion both pleasant and refreshing.

Another story tells of Daruma, founder of Zen Buddhism. He was meditating one day, but he began to drowse. In a fit of rage at his weakness he tore off his eyelids! oooooooooooh! He threw them down, and from the spot where they landed there grew two tea-bushes.

The first tea in Europe came from China. Portuguese merchants brought it home as early as 1559.

Tea was originally used for medicinal purposes, and was probably discovered by a herbalist.

The East India Company traded opium in exchange for tea!

China's Lapsang-Souchong Keemun and Jasmine teas are popular in the West. The well-loved Earl Grey tea is a blend of Indian and Chinese teas, together with oil of Bergamot.

Chinese tea-pots arrived in Europe during the mid-18th Century. The British pottery industry was able to expand based on the demand for similar pots, and then entire tea-services.

Original China teas are green. Our familiar 'black' teas are produced by the processes of withering, rolling, fermentation and firing. Green teas do not undergo fermentation before firing.

Confucius say... "If the stranger say unto thee that he thirsteth, give him a cup of tea."

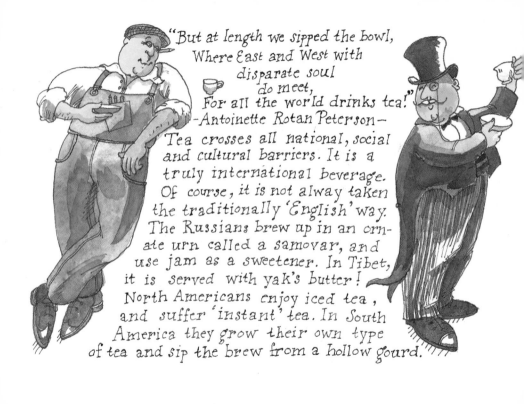

"But at length we sipped the bowl,
Where East and West with
disparate soul
do meet,
For all the world drinks tea!"
—Antoinette Rotan Peterson—

Tea crosses all national, social and cultural barriers. It is a truly international beverage. Of course, it is not alway taken the traditionally 'English' way. The Russians brew up in an ornate urn called a samovar, and use jam as a sweetener. In Tibet, it is served with yak's butter! North Americans enjoy iced tea, and suffer 'instant' tea. In South America they grow their own type of tea and sip the brew from a hollow gourd.

Tea Producing Nations

India
The world's largest Producer.

Sri Lanka
Tea makes up 70% of it's exports.

Kenya
Britain's third largest supplier

China
Tea's country of origin.

Uganda

Indonesia

Turkey

Russia

Argentina

In China...
Chia or Cha

In Italy...
Tê

In France...
Thé

In India...
Cha

In Russia...
Chaĭ

Old English...
Tay

In Turkey...
Chày

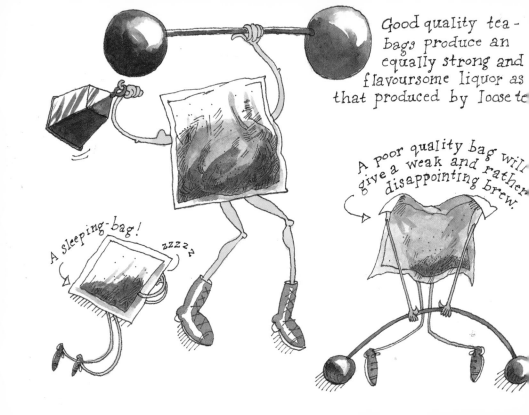

Good quality tea-bags produce an equally strong and flavoursome liquor as that produced by loose te[a]

A poor quality bag will give a weak and rather disappointing brew.

A sleeping-bag!

zzzz

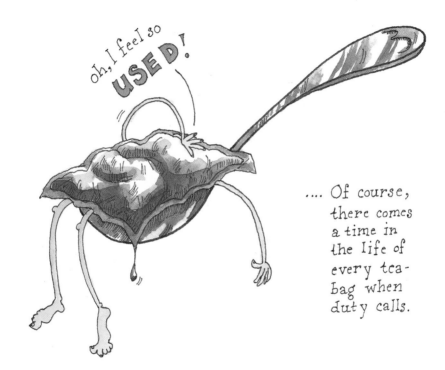

Put away the tranquillizers! Tea will cheer you up. The reason is mostly psychological but is partly due to caffeine content. This increases mental and physical powers when taken in small quantities. However caffeine being a stimulant, it is considered an undesirable substance by certain religious groups such as the Mormons and the Seventh Day Adventists who never drink tea. Poor dears!

Tea was originally considered as a medicinal herb, supposedly curing many ills. Hot sweet tea is a well used remedy today for mild cases of shock.

However, John Wesley the Evangelist and his followers did not agree. During the 18th Century they campaigned against tea-drinking for 12 years, until Wesley finally succumbed to the temptation of a long awaited cuppa! Perhaps it was during this time that Wesley's supporters first used the expression 'tea-faced,' which means to have an unhealthy pallor, like one addicted to drinking tea!

Japan

Tea-drinking in Japan was widespread 850 years before it was first seen in England. The preparing and partaking of tea became a symbolic and formal ceremony called "Chanoyu". The ritual was first outlined by Rikyu (1522-91). The green teas used for the ceremony are called Koicha and Ususha, the tea is sipped and then passed around, wiping the rim of the bowl first of course!

The essential items for this ceremony are a charcoal brazier, a ladle, a caddy, a bowl and a cloth.

It is a great honour to be invited to take part in a tea ceremony, not every Chang, Fu or Lee gets the chance!

How
To Make
Tea.
A Guide for
the
Beginner

Volume
XII

Best
Quality

For a single cup

A traditional 'Betty' pot from Staffordshire.

A tea-pot was put on display at the 1851 Great Exhibition that held 13½ GALLONS of tea!

13½ GALLONS!

FAT BOY

A 'thermal' teapot.

A Present from Brighton

Peep!

A Victorian triple-spouted Pot.

My Gran's U.F.O. kettle.

this is all getting too much for me!

Tea-tasting is a highly specialized business. Tasters work to ensure that we can rely on a similar flavour and appearance every time we buy a particular blend of tea. This is an especially difficult task since tea from the same garden can vary from week to week!

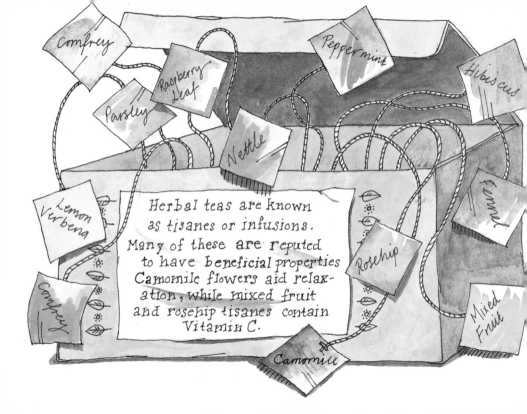

Of tea...

"Its proper use is to amuse the idle, relax the studious and dilute the full meals of those who cannot use exercise and will not use abstinence."

Doctor Johnson
(Who drank 40 cups per day!)

Rose plants love tea-leaves.

House-plants thrive on cold tea.

Stewed and strained, tea will clean glass and mirrors.

Denture cleaning tablets will clean up the inside of a stained tea-pots

Steep used tea leaves in a bucket for ½ hour, strain and use to clean wood before a final polish.

A storm
in a tea cup

Tea with milk contains **19** calories, but lemon tea is calorie-free! In America, iced lemon tea is very popular, served with a sprig of mint. Sugar in tea adds about 28 calories per spoonful.

lemon·tea

Tea was first taken with milk in 1655.

SUGAR *and other sweeteners*

Granulated SUGAR

To make sugar cubes, moist crystals are pressed into moulds and then dried.

Like tea, sugar used to be very expensive and so honey was used instead.

Saccharin

fruit sugar (fructose)

Sugar Daddy.

Brownies are encouraged to develop their tea-making skills.

Tea Ice Cream

2oz dry tea
1lb refined sugar
1oz arrowroot
2 pints milk
10oz water

Boil the water and warm a teapot,
put in the tea leaves and pour
on the boiling water, infuse for
8-10 minutes. Strain off the
infusion and keep aside
Boil milk, next blend the sugar
with the arrowroot and add to the
milk. Simmer for 10 minutes stirring
continuously to avoid lumps.
Remove from heat, add tea infusion,
stir and freeze.

PES

Tea Punch

For 12 people
½ pint strong tea
6oz sugar
½ pint orange squash
4 tblsps. lemon juice
2 small bottles ginger ale
1 large bottle lemonade
1 orange, sliced

Put the hot tea in a bowl,
add sugar and stir until
dissolved. Add the orange squash
and lemon juice and strain.
Chill.
Just before serving, mix in ginger ale,
lemon juice and orange slices.

Tea Jelly

2 lemons
1 pkt. lemon jelly
1 pt. fresh tea
whipped cream

Grate the zest of the lemons. Make up the jelly with the tea. Stir until dissolved, and allow to cool. When it has begun to set, stir in the lemon peel, and pour into a mould. (It helps to wet the inside of the mould with cold water first to ensure the jelly will come out again!) Decorate using the cream, a piping-bag and some inspiration!

Highland Fling!

2 measures strong tea
2 measures whisky
1 measure lemon juice
sugar to taste
dry ginger ale

Mix together all the
ingredients except the
ginger ale. Allow the
mixture to cool. Quarter
fill glasses with ice,
pour the mixture over
the ice until the glasses
are three-quarters full.
Top up with the dry
ginger ale.

'A nice cup of tea' and...

Come up and see me sometime "

A suggestive digestive?

hot buttered crumpets?

toast and marmalade?

MARMALADE

Sandwich 1½

an extremely fattening cream tea?

a jammy dodger?

United Kingdom

U.S.A.

Australia

Tea Imports

The Irish drink the most tea per person in the World. The United Kingdom comes a close second. It is the largest customer in the world, and the average Briton drinks **1,650** cups per year!

The first cup of tea in England, circa 1657. Drunk at the home of the Duke of Buckingham.

Property of No.10 Downing St.

That should keep one going for an hour or two.

British General and statesman the Duke of Wellington (1769–1852), was a great tea-drinker. He made sure he took plenty of tea with him on his campaigns.

The English Prime Minister William Ewart Gladstone (1809–1898), took his tea to bed in a stoneware hot-water bottle, warmed his toes.....and then drank it!

The Second World War brought the rationing of absolute essentials such as tea. The allowance was only 2oz per person per week. Tablets came onto the market that were supposed to make tea go 100 times further!

With the prospect of a gas attack, tea could be purchased in specially gas-proofed packages. However, it would have been

impossible to drink it whilst wearing a gas-mask!

At tea-time you would have been in the right place if there had been an air-raid attack. Strong, steel tables were available, that served as bomb-shelters.

Many different varieties of tea are available. Together with established favourite blends such as Earl Grey and English Breakfast there are, to mention but a few, lemon, orange, lime, apricot, peach, blackcurrant, even ginseng teas!

Fruit teas are ordinary teas flavoured with tiny pieces of dried fruit or a fragrant oil.

Cockney Rhyming Slang

Puzzled?
Thief........
'Tea - Leaf!'

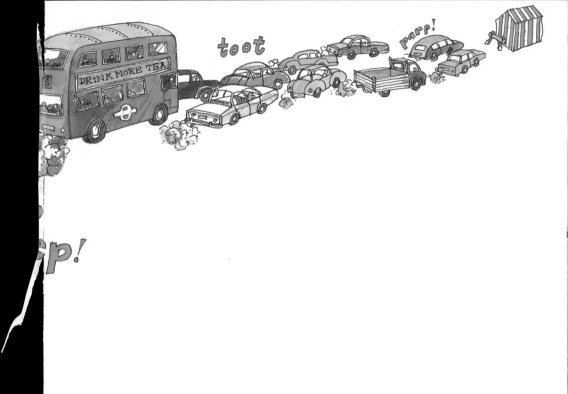